Bitter Sweet Love

Bitter Sweet Love

Michael Faudet

Andrews McMeel
Publishing®

a division of Andrews McMeel Universal

Andrews McMeel Publishing
a division of Andrews McMeel Universal
1130 Walnut Street, Kansas City, Missouri 64106

www.andrewsmcmeel.com

www.michaelfaudet.com

16 17 18 19 20 RR2 10 9 8 7 6 5 4 3 2 1

ISBN: 978-1-4494-8101-8

Library of Congress Control Number: 2016949279

The Fell Types are digitally reproduced by Igino Marini.
www.iginomarini.com

Cover art by Tinca Veerman
www.tincaveerman.com

Editor: Patty Rice
Art Director: Julie Barnes
Production Manager: Cliff Koehler
Production Editor: Erika Kuster

ATTENTION: SCHOOLS AND BUSINESSES
Andrews McMeel books are available at quantity discounts with bulk purchase for
educational, business, or sales promotional use. For information, please e-mail the
Andrews McMeel Publishing Special Sales Department: specialsales@amuniversal.com.

For Lang,

*I could watch a million sunrises and still never see one
quite as beautiful as your eyes slowly opening in the morning.*

INTRODUCTION

When I wrote my first book, *Dirty Pretty Things*, I found myself lost in a strange little world of my own making. Exploring the many facets of love and relationships, inspired by life experiences, nature, art, and often a bottle of vodka.

Like a well-constructed martini, the words seemed to flow effortlessly—gently stirred with each stroke of the pen.

And when the last sentence was written, I suddenly realized I had only just begun.

Bitter Sweet Love is a new departure point. A freshly dug rabbit hole to fall down once again, to a place where the sun refuses to set.

It is a book that continues to uncover the intricacies of love in poetry, prose, quotes, and short stories.

I like to think of it as an admission ticket to a beautiful but dangerous carnival ride.

One that races precariously along rusty rails which could snap at any moment.

I hope you enjoy the trip.

—Michael xo

CAN YOU REMEMBER?

I think you loved me,
　the night we drank
　Turkish coffees,
　our fingers woven
　tighter than two
　hands held,
　by lovers dangling
　on a precipice
　of a cliff.

Can you remember
　the moment
　our fingers let go?

The stars rushing
　backward,
　no hope left
　below.

CHASING LOVE

When chasing love
    at any cost—

The pathways meet
    but seldom cross.

I dream of dreams—

Once dreamt,
    now lost.

How sunshine steals
    from autumn frost.

WONDERFULLY RIGHT

I certainly know right from wrong, she said, but the trouble is, whenever I feel your hands unclipping my bra—wrong suddenly feels wonderfully right.

THE LETTER

Your words stirred something deep inside me, like a vodka martini sipped with thirsty lips——my body intoxicated by the very suggestion of you.

I read the letter again.

My hand between willing legs, writing a reply in cursive circles.

Upon pretty pink paper unfolded.

THE NORTHERN LIGHTS

She was like the northern lights on a cloudless night. Walking toward me, leaving a trail of dark footsteps on the silvery sand. The waves breaking gently behind her, white foamy fingers reaching out and caressing her ankles with swirling salty kisses. Beads of glistening water clinging to her naked body, dusty pink nipples hard, skin ghostly pale, a single strand of wet black hair curled like a comma across her blushing cheeks.

—

"I want you to fuck me," she whispered. *"It is far too beautiful an evening to make love."*

PROXIMITY

We joined the dots
   from A to B,
   the line we drew
   from you to me,
   traced empty shores
   across the sea,
   over mountain top,
   past forest tree,
   along the roads
   and walking tracks,
   all bridges burned,
   no looking back,
   for the love
   we have,
   no gate can stop,
   no barking dog
   or bolted lock,
   for what is real
   is meant to be,
   when two hearts
   beat—
   in proximity.

SLEEPWALKING

Lucy pulled up the creaky wooden blinds and peered out the rain-streaked windows.

It was a strange kind of morning.

Wispy gray clouds hung low over the old abandoned church. A sprinkling of watery sunshine touched the treetops of a little park across the road, and in the distance a gorgeous rainbow held the city rooftops in one hand and sparkling sea in the other.

She caught a casual glimpse of herself reflected in the glass.

Strands of straw-colored hair falling across her face, tickling her lips and almost hiding her sleepwalking eyes.

A trembling hand reached into the pocket of the heavy white dressing gown, searching for the cigarette she had long given up.

"Old habits die hard and new ones take their place . . ."

Something her shrink had told her at their last session.

She popped the pill into her mouth and walked over to the kitchen bench. Turned on the cold water tap and leaned her head over the sink.

It would be a while before the Ambien kicked in and heavy legs walked her slowly back to bed.

Just enough time to flip open the laptop, quickly check some e-mails, scroll through Tumblr, or maybe watch some Hentai clips and masturbate.

Flopping onto the couch, Lucy switched on the Mac and waited for the all-too-familiar windows to open.

A couple of cute cats, One Direction gif, a woman in pigtails being roughly spanked, and a F. Scott Fitzgerald quote rolled up across the dashboard.

Her fingers came to life, playing a concerto of hearts and reblog clicks, scrolling endlessly past image after image, until she stopped on a video that caught her twitching eye.

It was a homemade porn clip.

A girl in a yellow bikini was slumped down in a passenger seat of a car, baseball cap pulled down over her face. She was furiously rubbing herself, moaning, while the driver, a male arm to be precise, reached over and slid his hand under her top.

Lucy watched and slid a hand beneath her dressing gown.

The girl in the clip pulled her bikini bottom to one side, exposing her shaved pussy and started to slide her fingers in and out. Her head leaned back into the tan leather seat as she started to moan softly.

The familiar tingling and wetness started to tease and tantalize Lucy.

She quickly closed the laptop with one hand while the other hand kept busy. Closing her eyes, she lay down on her back, spreading her long legs a little, kicking a pillow off the couch.

Her mind slipped backward into a world of fleeting fantasies.

A shadowy figure pushed her knees apart and pressed his lips between her legs. While another stood over her, holding his hard cock to her mouth, pushing it in, fucking her open lips.

She cried out as the orgasm hit hard and fast.

Making her sit upright, fingers rubbing her swollen clit, hanging on to the last ripples of spasming pleasure that ran wild through her tense body.

Minutes passed before she could even begin to move.

When she did, each step took its toll, as heavy legs waded through the quicksand of Ambien-induced stupor.

The dressing gown fell silently to the floor, forming a puddle of white on the purple carpet.

Lucy leaned against the windowpane, eyelids heavy, opening and shutting like the graffiti-covered roller doors of a liquor store in a bad neighborhood.

It had stopped raining, and the rainbow was a faded memory lost to bright sunshine.

She could feel the warmth of the glass pressed up against her naked body. It felt comforting. Like a hug from a long-lost lover or a cat curled up under the covers of a bed.

"Old habits die hard and new ones take their place . . ."

The words did a slow waltz, around and around the empty dance floor, as the darkness descended deep inside her head.

Lucy tumbled down the rabbit hole again.

Where wonderland ceased to exist.

———

"Will you miss me when I'm gone?" he said.

"I will miss me," she replied.

REGRET

A memory picked
    from a flower wilted,
    its petals faded
    all color crushed.

How can I forget
    such fragrant perfume?

The lingering regret
    of a love long lost.

Wonderfully Lost

We slowly melted into a lazy summer of gentle sea breezes and singing trees. Each languid day rolling into the next like the curling waves caressing the silent sands. Our thirsty kisses sipping softly on wine-tainted lips as we fell quietly into each other's open arms.

Wonderfully lost and hopelessly in love.

THERE WAS A TIME

There was a time, not too long ago, when I spent my evenings chasing shooting stars with unanswered wishes.

My life spent curled up in an unmade bed.

Where dreams slept and reality awoke with each new morning.

These were the halcyon days of order found within the chaos of the seemingly unknown.

Each little metaphoric box ticked.

Every screaming kettle heard.

A cup of peppermint tea poured for one.

—

Now I live in a world of untied shoelaces, messy hair, and melting ice cream.

And all I can think about is you.

A Broken Heart

She stole my words
    I wrote with lips,
    a broken heart
    is seldom missed,
    by those who write
    another's name,
    upon the lips
    I loved—
    in vain.

Eyes Closed

Picking up the pieces of a broken relationship is like gathering up shards of glass with bare hands and eyes closed.

A WILLOW WEEPS

A willow weeps
    its tears run green,
    upon pages turned
    by rippling lake
    and drowning weeds.

A hooting owl
    in waving trees,
    a crying moon
    brought to
    its knees.

In falling leaves,
    an autumn spent,
    the love we found
    it came
    and went.

All parting words
    in darkness
    said,
    no rising sun
    can write anew—

For what is lost,
    a willow weeps.

INSOMNIA

I splashed the cold water across my face, the tap left running, my reflection in the mirror coming back to haunt me at 3 a.m.

The dark circles around my eyes had become angry whirlpools, pulling my sanity down into an abyss of utter exhaustion. A pale ghost sleepwalking to oblivion, each step sinking ever deeper into quicksand.

I had long given up counting sheep. The paddock was empty, the gate wide open, a lonely field where the sun refused to set.

I turned off the tap and watched the water drain from the sink, a fitting metaphor for what my life had become, before stumbling back to the meaningless sanctuary of an open MacBook Air that sat on a dusty kitchen table, next to a half-empty vodka bottle and a framed photograph of you.

Tired words tapped with yawning fingers, meaningless sentences typed one after the other, overwhelming me like unstoppable waves from a devastating tsunami.

No autocorrect could shake the shackles of my melancholia, fix the unfixable, or change the ending of this sad little story.

I opened the bottle and swallowed the inevitable sting of hopelessness.

Your beautiful smile, captured in the photograph, a constant reminder of an intoxicating love that once upon a time flowed endlessly, filling to the brim my now-empty heart.

Do you remember the afternoon we spent throwing paper planes off the cliff?

Folded love letters to each other, picked up by the wind, spiraling in the summer breeze, lost in a fleeting moment of dazzling sunlight.

The warmth of your lips pressed up against my neck.

My fingers running through your hair.

A hint of lavender, the slow drone of an airplane flying away in the distance, waves crashing onto the shore, ever silent, like a white carpet rolling onto the black sand below.

I wish I could forget it all.

Erase the past in an instant, hit the delete key, and open a new page.

Anything to escape the relentless surge of a miserable tide that swept me away each morning, only to drown me in sorrow come nightfall.

If only I could sleep.

Find solace in the darkness, collapse into a world of distant dreams and pitch my tent.

On that cliff top of singing flowers and lazy bumblebees.

Throwing paper planes forever.

OUR AUTUMN CAME

Our autumn came
    in coffee cups,
    from clouds of white
    to swirling brown,
    all wrinkly leaf,
    on muddy ground,
    the sugary sweet,
    sipped and stirred,
    with silver spoon
    and parting words,
    a butter knife
    on buttered toast,
    a morning mourned
    with marmalade.

No fond farewell
    in silence made,
    just falling tears
    in fallen rain,
    all sunshine gone
    no warmth remains,
    in empty cups,
    our autumn came.

HER KISSES

Her kisses were the wings of butterflies, beating softly upon lips of crushed petals—the perfume of love.

A Snowflake Falls

A snowflake falls,
   a story told,
   its melting words
   were mine to hold,
   I thought of you,
   when hands
   were held,
   two lovers lost
   to time
   it tells.

SWANS IN THE PARK

It had been a most peculiar evening.

Like riding a roller coaster in some broken-down carnival, never really knowing whether the rusty rails would snap at any given moment.

Vodka had helped smooth the ride.

Making some weird sense of it all, but ignoring the insanity of the girl that danced in her underwear to old Roxy Music songs played on a dusty turntable.

A half-smoked joint in one hand and a pair of dressmaker's scissors in the other.

We never made it to the bedroom.

Sassy had other ideas. Which involved black masking tape, a dining room table, and a vibrator shaped like a serpent.

"Think of it as a warm up," she said, wrists bound and legs spread across the hard wood.

Her moans becoming one piercing scream when the orgasm hit.

Followed by desperate pleas from pretty lips to fuck her senseless.

—

I awoke to the purring of a ginger cat pawing my face.

My back stiff from lying on the carpet, a head full of squeaking bats and eyes half open.

Sassy was standing over me, grinning, her long legs straddling my chest, a stick of pink cotton candy hovering over my startled face.

"What are doing?" I asked in a raspy morning voice.

"I've made you breakfast, darling. Bon appétit!"

I took the sticky cotton candy from her outstretched hand and watched as she sat down on the green leather armchair opposite me. Naked except for the red cape that covered her pale white shoulders.

"Hurry up and eat that," she hissed. "We have a big day ahead of us. Those swans won't feed themselves, darling. We've got to get down to the park before this storm passes."

I slowly rose to my feet, legs trembling and a sudden rush of vertigo sweeping across my aching body.

"I need to take a shower," I muttered.

Sassy leapt out of the chair, wrapped her arms around me, and kissed me hard on the lips.

"There you go," she said. "All nice and sparkling clean."

"You really are a terribly strange girl," I replied, trying to escape her vicelike grip.

"Oh, I'm quite mad," she laughed. "A runaway circus on acid. Kiss me again, I dare you."

———

We huddled by the murky pond, flashes of lightening exploding in the dark skies, a fierce rain soaking us to the skin.

A trail of bread crumbs drifting across the muddy water.

Two angry swans arguing over the last piece of stale crust.

HER EYES

Her eyes burn bright,
    all half moon glow,
    my shining stars
    in darkness lit,
    a welcomed light
    in stormy sea,
    when torrid waves
    crash over me.

No dancing fireflies
    can compete,
    all beauty found
    in eyes that meet,
    each curling lash
    unfurled, complete—
    her eyes in mine
    the love
    we speak.

PARACHUTES

The months passed.

My tears drying in the afternoon sun, all memories seeping into the shadows, the whiskey bottle empty.

The last phone message played, replayed, and played again.

Listening for clues.

Perhaps a hesitation in your voice.

Something, *anything* . . .

Nothing.

A magpie flew overhead.

Giggling children ran circles around a lonely tree.

A lawn mower sang in the distance.

All life returning to the park as I deleted your number with fingers numb and trembling.

—

We all make mistakes.

Mine was falling madly in love and forgetting to pack a parachute.

42

The universe
        its mystery held,
        by winking stars
        and magic spells,
        a milky way
        of frothy milk,
        all spinning spun
        its secrets spilt,
        by laughing moon
        and smiling sun,
        a hologram
        since time begun.

Where Alice lives
        in Wonderland,
        and rainbows made
        by sleight of hand,
        the open door
        we enter through,
        with golden key
        is 42,
        for what is real
        is real,
        is not,
        a riddle lost
        to a truth—
        forgot.

FEMME FATALE

She unclipped the pretty black bra and flashed me a wry smile.

Her eyes possessed that rarest of qualities, a sparkle of mischief with just a hint of danger.

And when she spoke, her words circled me, like hungry wolves moving in for the kill.

—

"I can't stop thinking about last night," she whispered. "I felt like a pinball machine. Your fingers hitting all the right buttons, bells ringing, my body lit up and begging for a replay."

My Heart

My heart has become a broken compass. Every time I try to leave you, I always find myself running back into your arms.

THE GARDEN

A lone sparrow hopped across the moss-covered table, stealing a crumb that had fallen from my plate, before darting back into the sky with a fluttering of speckled wings.

I took another bite from the slice of lemon cake, a bee buzzing past my ear, racing off to join the others feasting on a row of fragrant honeysuckle.

Miriam sat opposite me, sipping on a generous gin and tonic, eyes blank and smile missing.

A hushed whisper rippled through the trees, a quiet discussion between waving leaf and wispy summer breeze.

A deafening pause in our broken conversation.

I reached for my glass, the ice jangling as I emptied it, my mind desperately searching for the right words, any words in fact, that might make some sense of it all.

"I'm sorry."

Miriam gave me a sad little look, one that said all the words I should have said.

She slowly eased her way out of the creaking cane chair and straightened her floral dress with a soft brush of slender fingers.

One last glance in my direction.

Her parting words the last I would ever hear from those pretty lips.

—

"When we plant weeds in a beautiful garden, it is often tears of regret that water them."

THE BED WE MADE

A bed we made
    of thorny sheets,
    of jagged rocks,
    a chasm deep,
    cruel words once said
    a mountain steep,
    cannot be climbed
    in restless sleep,
    a nightmare shared,
    now ours
    to keep,
    for what is lost—
    tired eyes
    will weep.

THE GYPSY GIRL

The darkness descended like a black velvet shroud, silently covering the arthritic branches of twisted trees and decaying leaves as I stumbled blindly along the little earthy track. My face scratched by cruel thorns as I fought my way deeper into the dying forest.

I had been warned by the local villagers to stay well away. Hushed words whispered in the warm glow of burning embers, punctuated with furrowed brows and trembling voices.

Yet here I was, driven onward by vodka, drawn to disaster by the tyranny of conceit and reckless curiosity.

Suddenly a pinprick of light appeared in the distance and I felt a strange, tingly wave of excitement wash over me.

Little shocks of electricity flowing through my veins, making my heart beat faster.

—

I had often read about gypsy campsites in old dusty books that slept peacefully on the shelves of forgotten libraries.

Strange places where fires burned bright and crying violins told melancholy tales, laced with magic and mystery.

Immersed in the late-night stories of gorgeous gypsy girls wearing brightly colored silk and jangling jewelry, dancing wildly around the flickering flames.

However, what I found in the small forest clearing was an abridged version.

A single sentence written with a lone lantern that hung above a solitary door made of wood and tarnished brass hinges.

"Hello, anybody home?"

The words sounded ridiculous, escaping my lips before I had the chance to stop them.

Leaving me feeling awkward, my hands restless in the pockets of my coat, numb fingers doing their best to hide from the cold.

I didn't have to wait long for a reply.

A small sliver of light appeared, turning quickly into a triangle of red, before illuminating the trees on either side of me in a pale shade of crimson.

My eyes transfixed on the caravan door as it opened wide, revealing a magnificent vision that was to haunt my waking dreams forever.

She stood before me.

A waterfall of red hair falling carelessly across bare shoulders, a curvaceous body held hostage by a tight emerald-green corset, her scarlet lips framed by dangerous eyes and heavy black mascara.

When our eyes met, all time ceased to exist. The dying seconds frozen like the petals of red roses kissed by autumn frost.

I had never believed in love at first sight.

Until now.

———

I felt the silver dagger plunge deep within my chest, the orgasm still rippling through my naked body, the intense pleasure masking the pain.

A faint smile upon my lips.

As I watched the gypsy girl steal my heart with bloody fingers and place it into the tiny gold cage that swung above her bed.

Where it remains to this day.

We Spoke

We spoke of love
    and cities found,
    of buried gold
    deep underground,
    how rivers sigh
    when lost to sea,
    of whiskey poured
    in cups of tea.

We spoke of art
    in golden frames,
    of memories lost,
    forgotten names,
    how shooting stars
    write wishes bright,
    and shadows fade
    into the night.

We spoke of wolves
    and many things,
    of ticking clocks
    and circus swings,
    how crying doves
    fly up above,
    but most of all
    we spoke of love.

A Tragedy

Falling so madly in love with you is a tragedy. Nothing in my world will ever seem so beautiful again.

We Wrote

We wrote about love—our sentences the hands that caressed each other on warm summer nights. A story without an ending, written by a pen that would never run dry.

It Was Love

There was no fanfare or fireworks show. Just a quiet knowing somewhere deep within my heart. It was love and she completed me.

ANOTHER YEAR

Another year,
    a new beginning,
    a resolution made—
    to fall again
    in love
    with you—
    forever
    on this day.

IN TWILIGHT SKIES

In twilight skies
    we walk alone,
    to the dulcet beats
    of death's metronome,
    a passing cloud
    beneath our feet,
    all starry-eyed
    our world complete.

No falling tears
    from smiling eyes,
    no rainy days
    the puddles dry,
    this heaven found
    with life's release,
    in happiness
    we dance
    in peace.

In twilight skies
    we walk alone,
    to the dulcet beats
    of death's metronome,
    a passing cloud
    beneath our feet,
    all starry-eyed
    our world repeats.

NO REGRET

You were my beautiful mistake and I don't regret anything.
I would do it all again in a heartbeat.

MIAMI

It was another beautiful day.

A wonderful afternoon to be exact. All brilliant blue skies with a gentle touch of warm sunshine teasing and tickling the cool winter air. Not that it ever got really too cold here. There were only two real seasons of note, or so it seemed to me. One of which was apple-pie-oven hot and the other, a rather good imitation of a straight-from-the-fridge dark chocolate mousse.

Water was bottled. Palm trees lined boulevards. The sea always sparkled and ridiculously fit girls with sun-bleached locks roller bladed along the crowded foreshore.

How I ended up in this margarita-quenched Beach Boys utopia is another of life's wacky conundrums. Why I decided to rip up my return ticket and stay was far less of a mystery.

Like countless other romantic fools before me, I had succumbed to the oldest of boxed chocolates and flower bouquet clichés. I was hopelessly in love with a girl. Her name was Venus and she worked across the road in a bar that boasted sixty different types of tequila.

We had fallen into each other's arms three months ago to this day, one night after closing time at the bar, drowning our collective sorrows with endless chinking of shot glasses.

It was a predictable ending to an extraordinary evening. Venus moaning, miniskirt hitched up, blue panties pulled down, her back pressed up against the storage room wall, as we fucked to a dawn chorus of singing birds and waking cicadas.

A week later I had packed up my suitcase, checked out of the hotel, and moved into her one-bedroom apartment with balcony overlooking the beach.

Domestic bliss and a loved-up couple routine quickly followed. Me writing during the mornings, she pouring drinks in the evenings. Our afternoons spent sitting on the dunes discussing the universe. Watching the waves write frothy sentences on the sand as glistening surfers jostled for position and wiped out in an explosion of thunderous blue.

Weekends were extra special.

Lazy punctuation points enjoyed with the blinds pulled down. Passing the time curled up in bed watching movies with a Hawaiian pizza and icy cold beers or fucking beneath a tangle of white cotton sheets.

"What a gorgeous afternoon," said Venus yawning as she handed me a coffee. My thoughts interrupted by this girl who held my heart in her slender fingers.

She sat down next to me and stared out to the sea with sleepy eyes, pushing my typewriter to one side to make room for her coffee on the tiny glass table.

"The radio said it might rain later," I replied, watching a seagull land on the balcony.

"Ha! I doubt it," she laughed, taking my hands in hers.

She was right of course.

Every second spent basking in the warm glow of her smile and sparkling blue eyes was a beautiful day.

Perfect, in fact.

—

"I have never felt the touch of falling snow," she said. "But like love, I know it exists. Somewhere."

SEASONS CHANGE

It was once our spring
    when lovers met,
    and flowers grew
    without regret.

The summer passed
    as summers do,
    a setting sun
    my love for you.

Each falling leaf
    a fallen tear,
    the autumn came
    with winter near.

Now all that's left
    of love is death,
    a story told
    with frozen breath.

A Beautiful Night

We lay on a bed of warm summer grass beneath a silent sky of sparkling stars.

Our naked bodies lit by a waking moon that yawned and slowly rose up above the stillness of a breathless lake.

My fingers gently tracing the letters of your name on wet skin.

Your lips pressed against my neck.

It was a beautiful night for falling in love.

—

"Nothing this perfect lasts forever," she whispered. "Even our closest-kept memories eventually turn to dust."

Petals

When our eyes met, all time ceased to exist. The dying seconds frozen like the petals of red roses kissed by autumn frost.

PEPPERMINT TEA

My thoughts were interrupted by an angel disguised as a sprightly elderly man, with a surprisingly well-groomed gray beard and one eye that always seemed half asleep. He wore a silver Rolex on his wrist (another surprise), and walked with an awkward gait that suggested some kind of old leg injury. Some would call him a stranger; I only knew him as Chris.

By now I knew the routine. A quick exchange of banter, which was always hard to follow due to his habit of discussing snippets of random wisdom, followed by an outstretched hand hoping for some small change or preferably a crumpled note from my pocket.

Today the conversation swung like a pendulum, between the influence of the Devil and the history of the Beatles. Not in any particular order of course, which made following his monologue just as confusing as ever.

I did my best to interact where I could, smiling in the right places and replying with a quick nod of my head or a hastily delivered anecdote that I hoped made some sense of it all.

Not that it really mattered to either of us, I guess.

It was more about the connection of strangers, a little oasis of warm humanity found on a chilly winter's afternoon.

Like always, between the talk of John Lennon and the temptation of Christ, rare uncut diamonds were uncovered. Dazzling bright in the watery sunlight of a rapidly setting sun.

"We live in an age of reduction," he said, "where hope and conscience has fast been whittled away by the blade of banality and stupidity."

Next to me, two Japanese girls started giggling and took selfies on their iPhones.

A businesswoman at another table sat stone-faced, staring blankly at her dying cappuccino.

The waitress, propped up against an outside wall, smoking a cigarette and crying. The café owner gesturing with hand signals, a mime that suggested she had done something wrong, again.

I poured some peppermint tea into a cup and watched Chris hobble back down the street.

My world getting smaller with every sip.

Rainbow

You are forever
my secret rainbow—

Beautifully written
upon a rainy,
gray page.

Where hope,
like love,
can be found again—

This gold
we share,
is ours.

WISH YOU WERE HERE

It was such a gorgeous day to end a relationship. All wispy white clouds and summer butterflies. Hands tightly held and then slowly released in the dancing shadows of warm sunlight.

I watched as you walked quietly out of my life with that familiar spring in your step. A quick wave good-bye wrapped in a sad little smile. The door left slightly ajar. A visual metaphor which would come back to haunt me over the next few months with every postcard sent.

You wrote about Paris, about your new life and how you missed me terribly on rainy nights.

Never once responding to my desperate pleas for you to return.

—

It's winter now.

As I walk alone across the frostbitten sand, my solitary footsteps writing a sad ending to what was once a beautiful love story.

My eyes stinging with salty tears.

As I look past the crashing gray waves toward a distant horizon.

My parting words lost to a howling wind.

—

"I have cried an ocean for you but still your ship refuses to sail."

BORDERLANDS

I am somewhere,
    strangely nowhere.

A lone comma,
    placed midsentence.

The worn needle stuck
    in a dusty groove
    of black vinyl,
    between the chaos
    and momentary calm
    of a Ramones track.

Standing still.

Where sea embraces shore
    and sinking sand rises
    to the farewell kiss
    of a crashing wave spent.

Always waiting,
    the seconds passing.

The anticipation of something,
    anything,
    forever calling.

Like the promise
    of a late-night
    Coney Island hot dog.

Dreaming of the moment
    when everything comes together,
    like melted butter
    and onions sizzling.

When mustard
    meets
    ketchup
    meets
    chin.

Lost is a lovely place
    to find yourself.

The Séance

I never truly felt comfortable leaving the sanctuary of my self-imposed solitude. Living alone in the little stone cottage by the sea suited me. Not that I was really ever alone. I had my library of books, a tired typewriter, a case of vodka, and a lazy Burmese cat to keep me company.

So what had driven me to leave the warmth of a well-lit fire?

Venturing outside was in itself an uncomfortable mystery. One that was fast unraveling with every heavy step taken.

—

It was a dreadful night.

Bitterly cold and gripped tightly by a blizzard of swirling snow.

I had a feeling of utter dread as I walked up the dark lane to the old house with the red wooden door.

Something deep inside me, a creepy-crawly fear that clawed deep within my stomach, told me not to knock on the door. *Better to run now,* it said, *far away and never stop running.*

Too late.

Even before my gloved hand had a chance to make contact, the door was opened from the inside and a smiling woman with flame-red hair stood facing me.

"Come on in, you must be freezing," she said, with a voice that seemed to sing the words rather than speak them.

The room was small and lit by flickering candlelight. A coal-burning fire glowed in the corner where a sleeping dog slept, curled up on a crimson rug. The woman took a seat at the round wooden table that stood in the middle of the space and gestured for me to join her with a sweep of her hand.

I unbuttoned my coat, hung it on the back of the chair, and sat opposite her. Taking off my gloves and rubbing my hands, trying to resuscitate numb fingers back to life.

"Do you believe in ghosts?"

It was one of those random questions that only the strangest of strangers could possibly ask but one I had kind of expected.

"I not sure I believe in anything anymore," I replied, my eyes meeting hers, noticing for the first time the intensity of green that outlined her black pupils.

The letter I had read just a couple of days ago, my admission ticket to this unsettling journey, had been signed by her hand, written with scarlet ink, revealing a name I was destined not to forget.

Ruby West leaned over and took my hands in hers, the silver rings on her long fingers digging into my skin. She spoke with hushed tones.

"It matters not what you believe or not, for tonight will change everything."

—

I was in love.

Walking along the empty beach, our laughter floating away in the warm breeze that swept across the sand dunes. Lucy's hand holding mine, her head resting on my shoulder.

A golden orange hue caressed the ocean, the sun melting slowly on the horizon.

It was a moment captured in my memory, more vivid than any photograph could possibly tell.

An image that came back to haunt me.

A petty revenge played out countless times in my tortured mind.

All happiness lost with a swift stroke of a razor blade by a girl possessed by melancholia and sleeping pills.

If only . . .

—

The letter had a trace of perfume, what seemed like a faint hint of lavender, and the handmade paper was tied with a black ribbon.

I had read the words quickly, then reread them again slowly, each sentence stabbing my heart and making the hairs on my neck stand to attention.

Who was this Ruby West? How could she possibly know? What did she want from me?

My instinct told me to burn it.

Throw the wretched thing into the fire and forget about it.

Instead I reached for the bottle of vodka, tears streaming down my cheeks, my thoughts turning to Lucy and everything that had been lost in the passing months since her suicide.

How could I resist the invitation written in scarlet ink across the page?

A broken man desperately searching for answers.

Clinging on to a tiny fragment of hope with trembling fingers.

—

Ruby's head fell backward and a guttural scream erupted from her lips.

The dog started barking, a painting fell from the wall, and I could feel my hands trying to escape her grip but unable to do so.

I didn't know what to expect from the séance but it wasn't this.

A flame from one of the candles suddenly burst upward, an explosion of eerie light bouncing along the cracked ceiling.

Sheer panic embraced my shaking body and the air in the room turned icy cold.

"I've missed you, my love."

It was Lucy's voice.

Her blue eyes meeting mine as she lifted her head, red ringlets falling across her forehead, the familiar smile now sitting across from me.

She was dressed as I last remembered her from that day spent walking on the beach.

The pretty floral dress and the daisy chain I had made on that beautiful summer's day hanging around her pale neck.

I could hear the seagulls cry as the walls faded away and we fell into each other's arms on the sandy dune. My lips finding hers, our kisses hungry and deep.

"I love you," I whispered, my hand reaching inside the dress, feeling a nipple harden to the touch. Her back arching as she wrapped her long legs around my waist.

Nothing made any sense but I didn't care. Lost within the warmth of her body once again. Her delicate fingers slowly unzipping my jeans.

We fucked to the sound of crashing waves in the distance.

Her dress hitched up and yellow panties pulled down around one ankle.

Cheeks flushed and mouth open as she came, her body rippling with aftershocks of pleasure.

———

We lay on our backs, staring up at the clouds, the blue sky changing to orange.

"Why did you leave me, Lucy?"

It was the question I had rehearsed so many times in my head but somehow it now felt empty and almost devoid of any reason.

"I never left, my love, and I never will."

———

The cup of green tea was laced with honey and I drank it without saying a word.

I knew the séance was over.

Ruby prodded the fire with an iron poker, sending a procession of spiraling sparks up the soot-stained chimney.

She then turned and walked over to me. Her hands resting on my shoulders, the words tumbling from her lips.

"Love like death needs no explanation," she whispered. "It is the curse of being mortal."

MAY ANGELS SING

May angels sing
    a song,
    my love—
    a lullaby to sleep.

The life you lived
    lives on,
    my love—
    this heart is yours
    to keep.

A solace found
    in dying stars,
    shine on
    my love—
    shine bright.

DAYDREAMING

You destroyed me with lips thirsty for thighs and knees pushed apart. Strong hands my undoing, fingers firmly pressed into pale white skin. My mouth open, moaning, begging for ruthless kisses and hair pulled hard. Buttons ripped, black bra unclipped, my fantasy fulfilled in a field of blushing daisies.

—

"A penny for your thoughts," he said, gently brushing a lock of hair from my face.

"Oh, it's nothing really," I replied, looking up at the clouds.

RESPECT YOURSELF

Always fight for love—walk barefoot across the jagged shards of a broken heart but never become its victim.

PAPER PLANE

I wrote you a love letter to explain how I felt about us—
folded it neatly into a paper plane and threw it off a cliff.

The Beach House

I woke up to the sound of angry seagulls and the distant thunder of breaking waves.

My eyes slowly adjusting to the brilliant sunlight. Hypnotized by little diamond sparkles that bounced off an empty vodka bottle and the unfastened clip of a discarded pink bra.

"Good morning," Lucy said in a singsong voice.

She walked into the room, a trail of wispy bluish smoke, and handed me a water with freshly picked mint leaves swirling around inside the tall glass.

"Is it?" I replied, my unsteady hand searching for the packet of painkillers I kept somewhere in the creaky drawer next to the bed.

"Here, this will help," she laughed, passing me the last half of a glowing joint.

I forgot about the pills and took a long, deep drag, held the smoke in, and then blew a cloud of LA's finest hydroponic into the air. Lucy had a remarkable talent for tracking down the best gear and this stuff was scarily excellent. I could already feel the familiar smile creeping across my face.

"It looks like the magic is working," Lucy said smiling. She took the joint from my lips, leaned over, and pressed her lips against mine.

Her kisses reminded me of lemon slices drizzled with sticky honey. Bitter, sweet, and strangely irresistible.

Lucy hopped onto the bed, straddling me with her legs spread, the skimpy yellow bikini bottom resting against my chest. I watched, transfixed, as she reached behind her back and untied the matching top, letting it fall silently onto the sheets.

"Breakfast is served," she laughed.

—

We watched the sunset from the sand dunes, drinking beer and staring out to sea. The salty breeze gently tugging on Lucy's flame-red hair. She took my hand in hers.

"I live in a peculiar world," she said, "in a place where reality ends and fiction begins. Maybe that's why I love you."

VENUS

I can still remember the hot summer's night we sat by the lake, beads of water clinging to our naked skin, while a full moon rose from the shadows of swaying forest trees. My head resting on your shoulder as you pointed out Venus, our words whispered, a love story written by stars.

—

"When you look into my eyes, what do they say?"

"I'm obsessed with you. Utterly, willingly, and wonderfully so."

A LOVER'S TOUCH

To feel your hands
    upon my skin,
    a lover's touch
    from deep within,
    from gentle moans
    to piercing scream,
    a pleasure felt
    from here between—
    my legs adrift
    in joyful dream.

THE FINAL ACT

It was a farewell of sorts.

A slow good-bye played out on a sad little stage by lovers who had fast become bad actors.

All the words between us had turned to shallow snippets of dying dialogue.

Growing colder with each meager exchange like the coffees sitting untouched on the café table.

Uncomfortable silence punctuated by empty stares and unanswered questions.

I reached across and took your hand in mine.

All the years we had spent together suddenly swept away within a sea of untangled fingers.

A magnificent love lost forever in the familiar warmth of a parting embrace.

The final act before the velvet curtains came crashing down.

WE MADE LOVE

I think somewhere, in a parallel world, we made love in a garden of wilted flowers. Our trembling hands reaching out, trying to grasp the last watery rays of a dying sun. Where our hearts collided and shattered into a million tiny stars.

WE ALL DROWN

A trickle of silvery moonlight ran down her cheek. "We all drown a little," she whispered. "That's how we learn to swim."

MIDNIGHT IN MANHATTAN

A quiet sigh escaped from scarlet lips.

Sophia loved the caress of lingerie on her skin——the secret thrill of hard nipples pressed against black lace.

Her reflection a ghost in the moonlight, haunting a rain-streaked hotel window.

———

Sophia turned around and smiled.

She watched as Serena unzipped her tight leather red dress and let it fall to the floor.

"You seem happy to be back in the city."

"I am. Very much so," Sophia replied, walking slowly over to Serena and kissing her hard on the lips.

Serena slid a hand between Sophia's long legs, feeling the wetness beneath her pretty panties.

Sophia sighed again.

—

"I love New York. The perfect place to read books, people watch, and fuck to the sound of sirens screaming late at night."

LOVE

Falling in love is not rational. It's madness. A beautiful, wonderful moment of magnificent insanity.

SUNDAY IN BED

"Atoms can never touch," she said.

I reached out across the bed, taking her hand in mine, pressing it up against my lips.

"When you bring them together they reach a point where they start to repel."

"How sad it must be for two atoms that fall in love," I replied.

Lucy smiled and kissed me hard on the lips.

"Oh, I think that changes everything. It always does."

THINKING OF YOU

I traced a raindrop with my finger as it slid down the windowpane, thinking of you and our final good-bye.

CHERRY BLOSSOM

Pink cherry blossom falling,
    I often wonder why,
    a beauty slowly taken
    like branches now forsaken—
    I am the tree
    that learned to cry.

Farewell my love,
    to fallen love,
    the wind became
    your words,
    the emptiness
    between us,
    the silent petals
    upon the earth.

Sunrise

A leg outstretched, the gentle stirring of crisp white sheets, a brilliant sliver of orange glow peeking through the bedroom window.

Pretty lips waking, a soft sigh lost to forest birdsong.

I could watch a million sunrises and still never see one quite as beautiful as your eyes slowly opening in the morning.

MY LITTLE LIGHTHOUSE

I could speak of many things.

How she lights up a room whenever she enters.

The brilliance of her smile when flashed in my direction.

The warm glow of her body lying next to mine on stormy nights.

The radiance of her presence when the darkness descends and all hope seems lost.

I call her *my little lighthouse.*

THE MIRROR

Miriam stared at the reflection in the mirror and barely recognized the woman who looked back.

Somehow the years had slipped by without her really noticing until today.

Gone was the young girl who fumbled and fidgeted in class, chewing on the end of a pencil, dreaming of falling in love and touching herself under the covers.

Missing too was the awkward girl who had stupidly said "I do" a couple of years later.

Even the confident girl who had recently found fame and fortune in the art world, had decided to pack up her brushes and run away to somewhere.

Miriam took a closer look.

Her distinctive black bob was now streaked with wispy strands of silvery gray and the fine lines that framed her smiling eyes told a brand-new story.

She was happy.

No longer shackled to the impossible dreams of youth and worldly expectations. The husband long gone and the white picket fence smashed forever.

For the very first time in her life Miriam felt blissfully content, empowered, and wonderfully free.

"Come back to bed."

Lana's words floated across the bedroom, wrapping themselves around Miriam's naked body with a warmth she had never experienced before.

Turning away from the mirror, the girl finally became the woman.

At peace with herself and madly in love.

LILY

We all live with the burden of at least one regret.

Mine was called Lily.

Her final words etched into my memory.

—

"Many a beating heart is silenced by the tyranny of indifference."

A BELL DOES SING

A bell that tolls
    with singing chimes,
    confetti rain
    from brilliant skies,
    your hand in mine
    is ours to keep,
    the vows we said
    I do, begin—
    the love we grow,
    from deep within,
    on finger placed
    a golden ring,
    no rising sun
    shall set again,
    for joyous day,
    a bell does sing.

IMPERFECTION

I have always found beauty in the crooked and flawed.

A lone dark cloud dancing on a stage of brilliant blue.

The honesty of a song sung slightly out of tune.

A pretty pink scar, its story told in a sentence written on a milky white thigh.

I think that's why I love you and all your little eccentricities.

The exquisite poetry of imperfection.

Beautifully broken.

And wonderfully damaged.

MADLY IN LOVE

It had been a month now since I had first bumped into Lucy at the village carnival. Literally.

Her hot dog flying out of her hands, hitting my white shirt and spilling buttery onions, ketchup, and bright yellow mustard all down the front of it.

She was beside herself. Waving her hands in the air and almost dancing on the spot.

"I'm so sorry," she nervously cried. "I wasn't looking where I was going. Oh no, look at your shirt, I'm so very, very sorry."

"It's okay," I lied, reaching for a crumpled tissue from my hip pocket.

"No, let me do that," she said, taking the tissue from me and doing her best to clean up but making matters worse as she rubbed the stain deeper into the fabric.

I had to laugh. Watching this wisp of a girl with red hair and a crooked fringe try to navigate her way through what was nothing less than a bloody disaster. However, it was the moment the ice was broken, as laughter suddenly erupted from her pretty mouth and blushing cheeks.

Later that week, we met for coffee. Next, it was a movie, and before we knew it, we were sitting across from each other at a candlelit dinner, sipping red wine and eating pasta.

It fast became a spilt milk and broken teacup kind of romance.

A little manic, a lot of wringing of hands on her part, and several whispered conversations about nothing in particular.

Yet tonight it felt very different.

Lucy ran toward my waiting arms. Her green eyes burning bright, meeting mine with an intensity I had never seen before. She placed a finger to my lips, silencing any words that might tumble from them, before taking my hand and placing it firmly on her beating chest.

The seconds turned to minutes, the silence deafening.

Finally she uttered the words I would never forget.

—

"I'm a strange girl, hopelessly lost and terribly confused. What's worse, I think I may have fallen madly in love with you."

My Life Before You

I can remember a time when time itself seemed endless.

The second hand of a clock ticking in slow motion, the hour hand barely moving at all.

A dull, rhythmic monotony, filling an empty void of nothingness.

My life before you.

Now time has turned from a trickle to a raging river.

Bursting its banks with every beat of your heart.

Our love swept along by the rushing cold water.

Each passing day passing—

Into the past.

ECLIPSE

A solitary tear ran slowly down her cheek.

Reminding me of the painful words I had said, each syllable drawing a tiny bead of blood, making me feel pinpricks of regret deep inside my broken heart.

It was like our love had suddenly been captured, held for ransom by the eclipse of a dying moon.

A darkness cast, stealing the luminosity and innocent wonder from her firework eyes.

We found ourselves in the realm of suffocating shadows, sitting silently and staring out to sea.

Two shooting stars that had burned too brightly leaving a trail of sparkling nothingness.

—

Forgiveness came with a breaking wave, a gentle sigh, melting into the warm summer sand.

As the moon returned.

Its brilliant glow reaching out and guiding our souls along a pathway to redemption.

I felt your hand quietly take mine.

Your fingers tracing a new beginning, a smile drawn on the inside of my palm.

The universe had spoken.

SOPHIA

What do you want to do today?

It was one of those questions you dread, especially after an evening spent destroying a damn good bottle of Russian vodka and waking with a hangover that could demolish a large building.

I took another look at the text with blurry morning eyes and decided to play dead for a few minutes longer before responding.

No such luck as the next text pinged on my phone.

?????????????????

Sophia wasn't the kind of girl to let sleeping dogs lie or have texts go unanswered.

Lunch, The Gallery, 12:30?

It was the best my trembling fingers could think of for a reply and perhaps a couple of coffee martinis might be the fix my fuzzy brain desperately needed.

Sophia's reply came lightning fast.

Yes!!!!!!!!!!!!!!!

———

I arrived at the restaurant like a man walking through thick mud.

The steaming hot shower and Red Bull had helped, but only just. Sophia was sitting at our favorite table in the corner, head down and scanning the menu.

"Sorry I'm late," I said, collapsing into the chair and summoning over a waiter.

"I hope it was a pleasant death," Sophia laughed, eyes locked on mine.

The Gallery was a darling of a restaurant. Small, cozy, and unassuming, apart from the million-dollar paintings hanging on the cream-colored walls.

The restaurant was the indulgent hobby of the owner, Malcolm Devlin, who had made his fortune as a Wall Street trader before relocating to London to pursue his hospitality ambitions. There were no reservations or casual walk-ins allowed. It was a membership-only affair, with guests carefully vetted and an annual fee paid that covered all the exquisite food and fine wines. A little like a time-share arrangement. Sophia's brushed metal card gave her entry for Wednesday lunch times and the coveted Saturday nights.

A coffee martini was placed quietly next to me while Sophia rattled off the order for both of us. Two dozen oysters to start, followed by the seafood platter for two and a bottle of Taittinger champagne on the side. The immaculately groomed waiter flashed her a smile and took the menu away.

"I thought I best handle the important decisions for the day," she smiled, leaning over and kissing me on the cheek.

I loved this gorgeous girl who had the delightful habit of drifting into my life at the most unexpected moments. Wild and unpredictable, ridiculously rich and with a heart of gold to match. The last time we had met was six months ago at Sophia's 30th, a dinner party that started with a birthday card and ended up in the tabloids. Celebrities and paparazzi fighting on the sidewalk.

"So how long are you in town?" I asked. "You know, it would have been nice to have had some warning. I would have gone easy last night and feel much better for it."

"Drink up," she replied. "You'll be right in no time."

I drained the last drop from the martini glass, only to have it instantly replaced by the grinning waiter. Sophia was intent on getting me pleasantly plastered it seemed. Which was always her motivation whenever we met.

"So come on, tell me, how long are you here for this time?" I asked again.

"Just the one night, on the red-eye tomorrow morning, heading off to Paris and then Milan," she replied.

The oysters arrived on a plate of crushed ice, seaweed, and sliced organic lemons.

"They're all for you," she smiled, reaching for a glass of freshly poured champagne. "Did you think I would buy you lunch without some pretty strings attached?"

The coffee martinis had kicked in and I could feel a mischievous smile writing itself across my tired face. "So you booked a room for later too," I said laughing.

Whenever we met in London it always ended up beneath the silk sheets of a messy bed in the Purple Palace, a small boutique hotel in Soho. Where discretion was served up nightly along with Belgian chocolates and a bouquet of bloodred roses. I loved the place and so did Sophia.

It was going to be a quick lunch.

———

"Untie me, please."

Sophia looked up, her green eyes sparkling in the candlelight. Wrists tied to the bedposts by sheer black stockings and a just-fucked wetness between her legs.

I did as I was told, my eyes never leaving hers, as I gently liberated each outstretched arm.

"We really should get married," I said, sitting down on the edge of the bed.

"Ha! Now wouldn't that be a hoot," she laughed. "The magazines would love it. However, I'm not sure Serena would be too thrilled with that arrangement. No, I think things are just perfect as they are, silly boy."

Serena was Sophia's longtime partner. Both enjoyed an open relationship and tolerated each other's little discretions as long as they didn't get too serious. More to the point, I really got on well with Serena and loved the nights we all spent together, drinking too much red wine and solving the problems of the world over a candlelit dinner table.

"I was joking."

Sophia sighed. "Really?"

It was a subtle hint of repressed regret that escaped her pretty lips and a deep down sadness I shared too, every time she walked out of my life.

I felt her arms wrap around me, pulling my body closer to hers as we fell into an embrace that seemed to stop all time in its tracks.

It was love and neither of us could deny it.

—

Returning home in the taxi I found myself staring blankly out of the window, taking in the early morning pantomime of sleepy pedestrians waking up to the prospect of another working day. Faces painted with grim expressions and heads buried in iPhones.

My mind drifted away to that magical moment when Sophia and I met for the first time at a garden party.

Both of us tipsy, doing a clumsy waltz around the circular dance floor, trying our best not to bump into the other guests but failing spectacularly.

Her head resting on my shoulder, the chemistry between us instant and intoxicating.

When the music stopped, Sophia smiled and looked into my eyes with an intensity that ignited a fire deep within my heart.

I can still remember the first words she spoke.

"I'm not the kind of girl who wants her name tattooed on your arm," she purred. *"Think of me as your dirty little secret."*

I Miss You

It was the day
    my world turned to dust.

The empty vase
    where violets grew,
    the unanswered text,
    a crumpled note
    cast to the floor—
    forgotten.

A saucer of milk
    left untouched,
    the familiar meow
    of a cat silenced,
    by a final click
    of a door closed—
    forever.

It was the day
    I held you for the very last time—
    like a desperate moon clings
    to a morning star.

GOLD

Love is the real currency—the true wealth we all possess. Spend it wisely.

WITH YOU

Whenever I'm with you,
   the clocks stop ticking,
   death is forgotten
   and spilt milk—
   stays spilt.

QUICKSAND

To speak of unconditional love is like building a palace on quicksand.

THE BOARDWALK

I often found myself wandering along the creaky wooden boardwalk that lined a sandy beach of setting sun and loved-up couples clutching last-minute ice creams. The dripping cones ignored between hurried kisses and selfie shots taken with crooked horizons.

A kaleidoscope of constantly changing images moving in time with each step taken.

A lone Ferris wheel turning slowly in the distance. The squawking of angry seagulls fighting over the last thrown french fry. A wispy trail of grayish smoke curling up from a group of huddled skaters, the sweet aroma of pot and half-eaten hot dogs. A gorgeous girl with auburn hair, reading a well-worn copy of *Brighton Rock*. An elderly man sitting next to her, wearing an olive-green suit and a sleepy white terrier lying by his feet. The muted thunder of crashing waves, sparkles of dappled light dancing across the restless ocean. Sugary doughnuts placed into pretty pink paper bags by the Polish lady who never smiled, her gaudy purple-and-green-striped stand surrounded by a bunch of screaming children.

Suddenly, something new but strangely familiar caught my eye.

A shop window, filled with dusty headless mannequins, dressed formally in chic vintage clothing and antique jewelry. The sign above the door said "Under New Management," written in red cursive lettering. A hypnotic trickle of Billie Holiday singing "Blue Moon," flowing from two tinny outdoor speakers.

Somehow I felt drawn to this place, an overwhelming feeling of belonging taking me by the hand and pulling me inside, or maybe it was just the codeine kicking in. I had taken two extra-strength tablets before leaving home. To calm a restless late-afternoon hangover and take advantage of that wonderful, almost detached, floaty euphoric existence that the little white pills conjured up.

A tinkling silver bell rang above my head as I pushed open the squeaky door and entered the shop. My eyes blinking, adjusting to the low light, slowly taking in the cluttered shelves and crowded floor space, filled with all manner of treasures and curiosities.

A statue of the Virgin Mary wrapped in flashing colored fairy lights stood silently in the corner. Wooden shelves lined the walls, filled with wonderful old books, pristine 1960s *Playboy* magazines, various pieces of poster art, unscratched vintage toys, and a taxidermy fox with an amazingly intact bushy tail. In fact, everything seemed in perfect, mint condition for its age.

Inside an ornate cabinet I noticed a butterfly collection pinned to a yellow canvas and enclosed behind glass, surrounded by a gold gilt frame.

It was sitting among a collection of novelty mugs, shiny tobacco tins, war medals, and pocketknives with bone handles.

I carefully opened the doors to take a closer look.

"Can I help you?"

A young woman appeared from behind a heavy red velvet curtain. She was dressed in a black and white vintage tuxedo, complete with silk top hat and shiny black patent leather lace-up boots. Her face was a shade of moonlight white, with dark circles around her pretty blue eyes and smiling lips painted purple. It was difficult to guess exactly how old she might be. Somewhere between mid-twenties and early thirties maybe. In her hand she held a lit cigarette.

"Oh, I was just checking out the butterflies, the ones in the frame," I replied, a little startled.

She took a long drag from the cigarette, blowing the bluish gray smoke upward.

"African. They're in good condition, too. No broken wings. Are you a collector?" she asked.

"No, not really, just curious. My grandfather had something similar—well, I think he did, many years ago."

Her eyes lit up and she stood to attention, clicking her heels and saluting.

"Hello, my name's Sabrina and I'm the owner of the shop. Welcome to my alternative world of fascinating yesterdays!"

The words were delivered with an upbeat, almost carnivalesque ring to them, her delicate hand outstretched, waiting for me to shake it, which I did. Her grip firm but gentle, silver rings covering three of her slender fingers.

I felt a tingling in my arm, which was both alarming and pleasant, like a mild electric shock mixed with a relaxing post-massage kind of buzz. Within seconds, this wave of electricity swept through my entire body, making the hairs on the back of my neck rise up.

"Ha! I'm sorry." She laughed, letting go of my hand quickly. "I sometimes have that effect on people." She turned and walked over to the counter and stubbed her cigarette into a circular brass ashtray.

Any thoughts of the framed butterflies quickly vanished, as I clenched my right hand and opened it, repeatedly, trying to rid my fingers of the weird pins and needles feeling.

Sabrina walked over to the front door, turned a key in the lock, and pulled down a black blind. She turned and flashed me a smile.

"I think you will be my last customer for the day. Anyway, there are far more thrilling things to do than make small chitchat about African butterflies and stuff."

"Well, I guess I should be on my way," I said awkwardly, not sure what was really happening in this strange little shop.

"No need to rush anywhere," she replied, reaching for my hand. "Come with me, please, I want to show you something pretty amazing."

She took me by the hand and started to lead me toward the back off the shop, past the counter and toward the red velvet curtain. I didn't resist or feel any more sparks of electricity, I just followed obediently like someone seduced by a dream, never wishing to wake.

The moment I emerged on the other side of the curtain the last thin shard of reality shattered.

—

My eyes were met with a blinding white light that faded in a split second, reminding me of an old camera flash exploding. Blinking furiously, the dark circles started to disappear and the sights and sounds of a café came into full view.

I found myself sitting at a round wooden table covered with a crisp white tablecloth. A cup of black coffee was in front of me, a croissant lay on a white plate by its side, and sitting across from me was Sabrina. The tuxedo outfit had gone and in its place was a striped tee and a short floral skirt decorated with daisies. A small black leather handbag hung from her chair. She picked up her swirling café au lait and took a sip, her eyes never leaving mine.

A cold panic gripped me and I felt my chest constrict, my mouth starting to grasp for air.

"Hush now." She laughed, putting her cup down and gently stroking the side of my face. "The adjustment is always a bit freaky the first time. It'll pass. See, you're feeling better already. Now drink your coffee and just relax."

I did as I was told and she was right. Somehow the first bite of the strong coffee sent a wave of calmness rippling through me. My heart stopped pounding and a pleasant sense of peace descended upon me.

I slowly became more aware of my surroundings.

Smartly dressed waiters zigzagging between the tables of casually dressed patrons, many engaged in noisy conversations, others hunched over a newspaper. Everyone seemed to be speaking French.

The more I turned my head and looked around, the faster I realized nothing made sense. Not the old cars whizzing along the narrow street or the vintage clothes worn by the pedestrians that strolled past me.

"1964, St. Germaine, one of my very favorite yesterdays. If you're not going to touch your croissant, I'll have it."

Sabrina didn't wait for a response. She took it quickly from my plate and started to devour it, the buttery, flakey crumbs sticking to her orange lipstick.

So many questions rattled around inside my head, each one seemingly ridiculous and insane. How can you possibly make sense of the impossible?

"I know what you're thinking," she said. "The hows and whys of it all, but believe me, you don't need to know. It just is. I can tell you this much, you will return to your world, but not before we've had a little fun in this one. Come on, let's get out of this joint and take a look around."

I followed her cue and stood up. Sabrina took some crumpled notes from her handbag and slid them under the plate.

The rest of the morning was spent ducking in and out of the various shops that lined the avenue. Bookstores, fashion boutiques, and cute little places that sold all manner of bits and pieces. It was a shopping trip, and it wasn't long before Sabrina was clutching several bags, filled to the brim with what she called "future merchandise."

"I can't resist a bargain," she laughed. "Can you imagine what I can charge for all of this when we return?"

That's when it hit me. The secret to her "alternative world of fascinating yesterdays" shop. Sabrina was a time-traveling entrepreneur who bought in the past and sold in the present. It also explained how the stock in her shop looked so new and in perfect condition.

"It's incredible. How do you do it? How did we travel through time? This is fucking crazy."

Sabrina gave me a quizzical look and then smiled. "No, silly, we didn't time travel anywhere. I just opened the door to a parallel world. There are many doors and countless worlds. I just happen to love this one. It's all about manipulating quantum physics really, when you know how, it's easy but far too complicated to explain in an afternoon. Just think of it as falling down a rabbit hole."

We stopped outside a black door of a narrow terrace house. Sabrina off-loaded the bags into my hands and fumbled around in her handbag. She took out a key and opened the front door which had a small brass number 42 attached to it.

"Come on inside. It's not much but I call it home."

I walked inside the short hallway which opened on to a small lounge room. The walls were painted an emerald-green color. Two brown leather chesterfield chairs and a circular coffee table sat on a carpet of lime green. I put the bags down on one of the chairs and followed Sabrina up a set of stairs that led to her bedroom and a bathroom with a rust-stained sink and a claw-foot bath.

She turned on the taps and placed a plug in the bath.

"Now, why not get out of those clothes and freshen up? I'll leave a dressing gown on the bed for you. Place your clothes outside for washing. Oh, and don't drain the bath, I'll use the water after you've finished."

I had long given up questioning anything and watched her walk out of the bathroom.

My naked body sank beneath the hot water. All traces of my hangover had long gone, replaced with a strange euphoria that swept over me. I closed my eyes and focused on a piece of verse, something that I had been struggling to finish.

Love is a rare rose, the perfume intoxicating—
picked by fingers oblivious to the thorns . . .

"I thought you might want this."

Sabrina's voice snapped me out of my thoughts, my eyes opening quickly and hands frantically trying to cover myself.

She was naked.

A bar of purple soap held in one hand and a glass of champagne in the other. I cast my eyes downward, trying not to look at her, the image of her pert breasts replaying over and over in my mind.

"Ha! I never took you for the bashful type and from the look of it, not every part of you is shy," she laughed.

I could feel myself getting hard and my hands could barely contain the erection.

Sabrina placed the glass on the floor and stepped into the bath, her long, milky white legs straddling me as she lowered herself into the water. I looked up into her gorgeous blue eyes and let out a deep moan as she took my hard cock with one hand and guided it deep inside her pussy.

The electricity I had felt when I first shook her hand in the shop returned. It was even more intense. She pushed her hips down to meet each thrust of my cock. Her arms wrapped around my neck as we fucked, hard and fast, sending splashes of water flying out of the bath. Sabrina's final scream bouncing off the bathroom walls. Her orgasm triggering a flash of blinding white light.

———

I was woken by the tickling of a small white terrier dog sniffing my face. My sleepy eyes opened and the old man in the olive-green suit slowly came into view, peering down at me.

"Are you all right, son?"

I sat up, my head feeling dizzy, and realized I was lying on the beach, my nakedness covered by a robe with a blue paisley print.

"I think I'm okay," I replied, looking up at the old man.

He gave me a polite nod and continued to walk along the sand, his little dog trotting behind him.

I started to brush the sand from my hair and noticed a large parcel sitting next to me. It was wrapped in brown paper and tied with a black velvet ribbon.

Suddenly my memory came flooding back to me. The shop. Sabrina. The café. A black terrace house. A tiny bathroom. Fucking . . .

And then nothing.

It was like time had been neatly compressed. The hours reduced to minutes. I was back to the reality of a setting sun that hadn't set. The waves breaking behind me, the boardwalk in the distance.

I opened the parcel carefully and discovered the framed African butterfly collection inside with a handwritten note attached to it.

I thought you might like this. A little something from another yesterday. Your grandfather was such a lovely man. Sabrina. xo

P.S. Come by and collect your clothes sometime.

A smile crept across my lips. As the missing piece of verse wrote itself in my mind. The final words written by another's delicate hand.

How can you possibly make sense of the impossible?

Perhaps you don't even try.

—

Love is a rare rose, the perfume intoxicating—
picked by fingers oblivious to the thorns.

A pleasure found
in the sweet pain of discovery,
and when it wilts
how can we refrain?

From bloodying our fingers—
again and again.

POSSESSED

You stole my life
and possessed me,
a body held hostage,
unbuttoned
and bound.

My beautiful surrender
a ransom paid—

With ruthless kisses
upon trembling lips
which utter
not a sound.

I Remember a Time

I remember a time when life was simple.

No grand expectations to weigh me down or the drudgery of responsibilities to hold me back. Living the cliché of *footloose and fancy-free*. A few jangling coins in my pocket for the morning newspaper and just enough notes by the end of the week to throw across a nightclub bar.

It was a hybrid existence of lectures by day and hanging out with good friends at night. Smoking joints in the shared apartment, listening to the mournful wailing of The Cure, and avoiding the razor-sharp claws of our resident crazy cat called Spooky.

Somewhere in between the playful chaos and outrageous laughter, there was also enough time to hold down a part-time job. Stacking supermarket shelves three nights a week.

Girlfriends came and went like the change of the seasons. The giddiness of love often replaced with the tears of regret, played out in my corner bedroom with the ebb and flow of powder-blue cotton sheets.

Of course, the years rolled by as years do. Friends drifted apart, more keys got added to the key ring, and Spooky slept soundly under a rose bush.

The Friday night happy hour was replaced with Saturday night martinis in flash restaurants, the names of which I struggled to pronounce by the time dessert arrived. The part-time job was left behind in the dust and a 60-hour a week career stole what was left of any imagination.

I found myself aboard a miserable train hurtling toward middle age and oblivion.

Little did I know then, a fellow passenger had other ideas, a very different plan for my life.

A Sunday morning phone conversation changed everything. Her words a siren's calling, forcing my hand to pull the emergency brake, bringing the spinning wheels to an abrupt stop.

We stepped onto the platform together, hands held and hearts beating.

And life suddenly became simple again.

ROOM 613

It was the start of a spectacular day.

A generous sprinkling of late autumn snow had fallen overnight, coating the jagged teeth of the mountaintops with a blanket of icing sugar whiteness.

Six ducks rose up from the surface of the lake.

The flapping of wet wings breaking the stillness of the crisp morning air as they soared upward into the brilliant blue sky.

I closed the terrace windows and slowly walked back toward the unmade bed.

As hotel rooms went, this was a great one. Spacious, tastefully decorated with contemporary Italian furniture, a shiny stainless steel coffee machine, and a fireplace with real flickering flames.

Even the bar was something special.

Far from being mini, the full-size fridge was well stocked with all the spirits you'd expect and wonderful boutique craft beers I'd never seen before. The side door filled with half bottles of French champagne, Grey Goose vodka, and wine sourced from the local vineyards.

Of course, all this luxury came at a ridiculous price.

A minor detail deftly settled by the outrageous and outspoken girl with dyed pink hair and matching lipstick. A close friend of mine with fringe benefits and a seemingly unlimited trust fund.

Flopping onto the bed, I reached for the room service menu and scanned the breakfast options.

Smoked salmon bagel with cream cheese, capers, and fennel shavings instantly caught my eye, as did the toasted ciabatta with truffle brie, drizzled with a lemon-infused olive oil.

Sophia wandered in from the palatial bathroom, beads of water clinging to her pale skin, a white fluffy towel wrapped around her waist.

"Perfect timing," I said. "What do you fancy to eat?"

Her hand reached beneath my boxer shorts, gently caressing my cock until it hardened.

"This," she replied, a mischievous smile lighting up her face.

—

"Why are you crying?" I asked.

Sophia stood at the window, the afternoon sun streaming into the room.

She turned and gave me a faint little smile before replying.

—

"I've always longed to turn the last page of a romantic novel but it seems my life is destined to remain a book of short stories."

The Park

We walked most mornings,
   a trail of bread crumbs
   in our wake,
   ducks diving in the pond,
   pigeons pecking
   on empty pathways,
   beneath a rainbow sky.

Sparkles of watery sunlight
   clinging to your hair,
   a head turned—
   your smile
   reaching out
   and touching mine.

Raindrops dripping
   from dying leaves,
   in the little park
   of make-believe,
   our secrets kept
   by bonsai trees.

SUMMER STORM

She was wild, unpredictable, beautiful, and dangerous. Impossible to resist. A summer storm in a bikini.

PERSIAN FAIRY FLOSS

Persian fairy floss
   pulled apart
   by sticky fingers.

Your laptop open,
   pupils dilated,
   a Hentai clip
   playing on a pillow,
   my hand
   between your legs.

A soft moan
   quietly spoken,
   from lips
   that swallow,
   the last piece
   of sugary sex.

THE RIVER BANK

It was a gin and tonic kind of lazy summer's day. Pleasantly warm with just a hint of lavender in the air. One of those languid, do-nothing kind of afternoons, sitting under the old willow tree; its weeping branches reaching out and caressing the cool waters of the muddy riverbank.

Morphine's slender fingers danced a gentle waltz through her sister's ash-blond hair, turning the wispy strands of silvery yellow into perfect braids that fell across bare shoulders of milky white.

Opium quietly took a sip from her tall glass, stopping only to wince when Morphine pulled a little too hard on an errant lock that had tried to escape her busy hands.

Heroin, the eldest of the three, blew smoke rings into the air, flicking the ash from the freshly rolled joint onto the soft blanket of grass. She instantly knew from the very first toke that this particular harvest from her father's latest crop was destined to be, using his words, *"a vintage year."*

"My turn, my turn, pass it over here, H," said Opium in her singsong voice, her arm outstretched and finger comically beckoning for the joint.

Heroin took another deep lungful of smoke before handing it over and reaching for the manuscript that sat beside her. A collection of neatly typed pages, all ring-bound and written by her esteemed father, who lectured in biology and botany at Spectre Hall University.

When he wasn't teaching and writing books, Professor Estrange spent his idle days focused on his real passion in life: growing rare orchids and cultivating mind-enhancing new strains of marijuana.

"Yummy, yummy, yummy," cried Opium, a crooked smile slowly creeping across her pretty face. She watched as a spiraling column of bluish smoke rose up from her rosy lips and faded into the gentle breeze.

None of the girls heard the footsteps and were pleasantly startled when Serena appeared from behind them.

"Well then, what do we have here? A pretty young wolf on the hunt for helpless lambs," said Heroin, laughing.

Serena drifted silently to the ground, her summer dress forming a pool of swirling white cotton upon the sea of green. Her slender arm wrapping itself around Heroin's naked shoulders, lips kissing lips.

"You two should get a room," sniggered Opium, blowing a large plume of smoke into the air.

"You're just jealous," Morphine replied, poking her sister hard in the ribs with a perfectly manicured finger. "Now sit still. I've got one more braid to do."

"Ouch! You can be such a fucking bitch, M."

Opium angrily pulled herself away from Morphine's busy hands and stood up. She took a deep toke on the dying joint and flicked it away, sending it spiraling into the river.

Heroin ran a finger gently down Serena's cheek, tracing a line across her wet lips, the two lovers completely oblivious to Opium's little hissy fit.

Morphine gathered up the empty glasses and started to pack them away in a wicker basket, along with the half-empty bottle of gin. The unwelcome visit by a determined wasp, hovering, landing, and hovering again, made Opium giggle.

"I hope it stings you," she said, laughing as Morphine tried to shoo the unwanted visitor away.

Serena glanced up at Opium and flashed her a smile. "How's tricks, O?"

"Well, I was all fine and dandy before my witch of a sister decided to break my ribs," Opium replied.

Morphine laughed and picked up the basket. "Time to leave these two alone. Come on, you cry baby."

Opium reluctantly took Morphine's outstretched hand and the two sisters departed silently, like two ghosts lost in a forest of swaying trees and humming dragonflies.

—

Serena watched the sun melt into the distance, the river taking on an eerie orange hue, painting the reeds with long, dark shadows. She was naked. The white dress folded neatly by her side, a pair of crumpled pink panties hanging on a branch.

"It's so beautiful here," she sighed.

Heroin was already dressed, a joint freshly lit, sitting cross-legged, one hand flicking through her father's manuscript. She looked up, took another toke, and blew a perfect smoke ring.

"Then why are you leaving? What's so important about New York, anyway?"

A flotilla of ducks glided across the water. Serena stared blankly at them. She could feel the tears starting to run down her cheeks.

"I love you, H, and perhaps I always will."

THE DIARY OF HEROIN ESTRANGE. JUNE 8, 1998

If my ink were tears, would this pen never stop writing?

I cannot begin to fathom the intricate nature of love, the endless "whys" and the cold reality of "because." My restless heart held ransom by circumstance, left to drown in a river on a perfect summer's day. The memory of your kisses still fresh upon my lips.

Can a blade not cut any deeper into my pale wrists?

Your parting words, my life flowing from me. The pain unbearable. Overwhelming.

Only the echo of your laughter left behind to taunt me, a constant reminder of the happiness we once shared. Your body entwined in mine, all warmth fading as the minutes turn to hours.

Oh, to be numb. To escape the cruel torment of such bitter sweet love.

There is no perfect ending to a relationship.

No magic formula.

Just a silent scream as they rip your fucking heart out.

A RABBIT HOLE

I have never been fond of farewells or good-byes.

So instead I'll invite you to fall down the rabbit hole again.

Hopefully, like a spinning revolving door, the pages will turn and our paths will cross once more.

Back to where the journey began at the beginning of this book.

I hope you enjoyed reading *Bitter Sweet Love* as much as I did writing it.

Please stay in touch and feel free to share your thoughts and photographs on my Facebook, Twitter, and Instagram pages.

Thank you so much for your kind support.

I truly appreciate it.

I write because you exist.

—Michael xo

ACKNOWLEDGMENTS

A big thank-you to my wonderful literary agent, Al Zuckerman. Your ongoing advice and support is always much appreciated. Thank you also to Samantha Wekstein and the rest of the team at Writers House, New York.

Thank you so much, Kirsty Melville, Patty Rice, and everyone at Andrews McMeel for making this book possible and taking it to the world. I am truly grateful.

A special thank-you to Tinca Veerman for her amazing artwork on the front cover. Just like the cover you did for my book *Dirty Pretty Things*, it is beautiful beyond words.

To Oliver, my amazing son whose wisdom exceeds his age. Thank you for letting me win (sometimes) at Uno. I love you more than all the stars in the universe.

Mum and Dad, thank you for always being there for me and building the best bonfires ever.

Much love to my gorgeous sister, Genevieve, who when she isn't saving lives is poolside helping Ryder win another gold medal.

To my delightfully mad friends. Now you know why I've been missing in action. Looking forward to catching up for a glass or six of wine soon.

And last but never least, a massive thank-you to all my readers.

INDEX

Join Michael Faudet on the following:

Facebook   Tumblr   Twitter   Instagram